The Mystery on Bleeker Street

The Mystery on
BLEEKER STREET

by WILLIAM H. HOOKS

Illustrated by Susanna Natti

Alfred A. Knopf · New York

Other Knopf Capers books

Man from the Sky by Avi
Rosie's Double Dare by Robie H. Harris
Running Out of Time by Elizabeth Levy
The Case of the Weird Street Firebug by Carol Russell Law
The Robot and Rebecca by Jane Yolen

This is a Borzoi Book
Published by Alfred A. Knopf, Inc.

Copyright © 1980 by William H. Hooks
Illustrations Copyright © 1980 by Alfred A. Knopf, Inc.
All rights reserved under International and Pan-American
Copyright Conventions. Published in the United States by Alfred
A. Knopf, Inc. and simultaneously in Canada by Random House of
Canada Limited, Toronto. Distributed by Random House, Inc.,
New York. Manufactured in the United States of America.

10 9 8 7 6 5 4 3 2 1

Library of Congress Cataloging in Publication Data

Hooks, William H
The mystery on Bleeker Street.
(Capers)
Summary: Ten-year-old Chase, his 78-year-old friend Babette, and
Babette's old dog help the police get to the source of some strange
events, occuring around the Star Hotel. [1. Mystery and detective
stories] I. Title. II. Series PZ7.H7664My [Fic] 79–28288
ISBN 0–394–94431–3 lib. bdg. ISBN 0–394–84431–9 pbk.

FOR EDNA,
my favorite cat person

Contents

The Mystery on Bleeker Street

1

An Odd Twosome

IT WAS a strange spot for a Christmas tree—right in the middle of an empty lot. Empty, that is, except for an abandoned diner where a family of stray cats lived.

The diner was an old railroad car that had at one time been a small coffee shop. But the owners had closed the coffee shop and moved out three years ago. Still, the diner was well occupied—by this big family of street cats. The head of the cat family was an old three-legged tom called Peg.

Chase Bellardo hung the last tin can on the scraggly tree. Old Peg hopped over to the tree. He gave the can a careful sniff, looking for food, no doubt.

Butterfly and Timid Freddy peeked their furry faces around the corner of the diner.

"Come on, Peg," called Chase. "The tree is for you and all the Bleeker Street orphans."

At the mention of the word *orphans*, Chase and his friend Babette broke out laughing.

"I wonder what Mr. McNulty would think if he knew who the 'poor orphans' were who couldn't afford a Christmas tree," cried Chase.

"Did you see his face?" asked Babette. "He was almost in tears when I told him all about the poor orphans. But I didn't really *lie* to him, you know. And, besides, he always has trees left over anyway."

"No, you didn't lie. But you sure made it sound like Peg and Butterfly and Timid Freddy and all the other cats were real kids. Babette, you'd be great on television."

Babette bent her head to one side, and smiled at the tree. "That's the most interesting tree on Bleeker Street. Why shouldn't the diner cats have a little something special for Christmas?"

"They'll have a great time climbing the tree and batting around the cans," said Chase. "You suppose the garbage men will let it stay?"

Just then, Peg took a swing at one of the cans.

"Humph. They never clean up around the diner. That tree is safe till Easter at least! Well, time to clear out now and let the cats enjoy their tree."

Chase and Babette continued their walk along Bleeker Street.

Bleeker Street leads right down to the river. It is one of the few streets in the neighborhood open to the waterfront. Maybe that's why there are always so many people moving back and forth. It is a pretty odd bunch of people, too, who move along the two sides of Bleeker. The street is full of unusual little shops that sell way-out clothes and old books and records. There are second-hand shops, and several gypsy families live in storefronts there. That's why Chase and Babette don't look all that strange among the regulars on the street. They sure would look out of place anywhere else.

Babette Brell is French, as anyone might guess

from her name. She's tiny for a full-grown woman, but you wouldn't overlook her, even in the Bleeker Street crowd. Not with her wildly curly hair—flaming orange, no less. But just in case you should miss the hair, you'd never overlook the way Babette dresses.

Her winter outfit is always done in layers. A great fur hat sits on top of that orange hair. The hat probably began life as a fur muff since it's open at both ends. Flowing out from under her fake-fur neckpiece is a blue velvet cape with red embroidery. Shooting out from the cape is a purple skirt. It's made of silk and it dances around her ankles.

Space shoes—those funny-looking shoes that make everyone look as if they've walked through mud—finish Babette's regular winter costume. Of course, lots of little chains and buckles and bracelets and earrings play hide and seek in her outfit.

Babette can usually be seen walking her old

dog Josephine in a beat-up baby stroller.

Now, if you've gotten the idea that Babette is some kind of young hippie you're dead wrong. Most of the crowd on Bleeker Street *is* young and hippie, but not Babette. She may be a bit different but Babette is also a very proper lady. And she's seventy-eight years old.

Now Chase is another matter. Chase is ten years old and looks very out of place on Bleeker Street when he's not with Babette. Regular American apple pie—that's the way he *looks*. He's got brown hair, a short snub nose, and he looks just like a million other ten-year-old boys. He's a guy in a Kid Power sweat shirt, beat-up blue jeans, and sneakers that look like his mother never found out you could throw sneakers into the washing machine. He does wear glasses, but so do a lot of other kids his age.

But the apple pie business about Chase ends with the way he looks. The way he acts is

another thing. First of all, Chase likes Babette's company over kids his own age. He'd rather explore Bleeker Street with her any day than wait his turn as a second-string player on the softball team. The other thing about Chase is that he reads a lot, mostly mysteries and books about magic.

It was his reading interest that brought Chase and Babette together over a year ago. Chase was thumbing through the secondhand paperbacks at the Black Witch Bookstore. He had just pulled out a torn copy of *Mysteries of the Occult*. Suddenly, an arm reached over his shoulder, and a finger pointed to the word *occult*.

"Know what that word means?" a voice behind Chase asked.

He turned and there stood Babette, looking like a character that might have stepped right out of a book called *Mysteries of the Occult*.

Before Chase could recover, the old woman said, "The occult is about magic and things you can't really see, but somehow you know they are just as real as real."

Chase knew what she meant. He couldn't have explained it in words, but he knew. For a few moments he couldn't say a word. The strange old woman seemed to hold him in a spell. Finally, he gulped and said, "Thanks. I think I'm going to buy this book."

After Chase bought the book, he and Babette took their first walk together, down to the waterfront at the end of Bleeker Street. They sat on the pier and talked for a long time about mysteries and detective stories and the supernatural. That was a year ago. They've been best friends ever since.

People on Bleeker Street still turn around and stare at the colorful old lady and the apple pie kid. They are likely to mutter something like, "I wonder if that kid is lost."

Chase doesn't hear remarks like that. He's usually caught up in what Babette is saying. And

Babette always has lots to talk about. Now, as they walked along, she whispered, "There's something strange going on at the Star Hotel down at the end of the block."

"Everything about the Star is strange," replied Chase, not picking up the bait.

"Stranger than usual," said Babette, holding back to see if Chase would nibble at this morsel. But Chase just kept walking.

"Things get squirrely around here every year at Christmas time. I noticed something night before last when I was walking Josephine past the Star . . . ."

"Hold it, Babette," Chase broke in. "What do you mean by 'things get squirrely'? Stop hinting around and tell me what you saw that was stranger than usual."

"Fair enough," laughed Babette. "That's what I like about you Chase; you treat me like an equal. Makes me feel young again." Babette gave Chase a knowing smile. "Would you like me to continue?"

"Continue!" cried Chase. "I'm sitting on the edge of my seat."

"We're *walking*," said Babette. "Chalk up one for me." Then she went right on with her story.

2

Something Squirrely at the Star

"OKAY, things get squirrely along this part of Bleeker at Christmas, especially at the Star Hotel," continued Babette. "Most of the regulars staying at the Star just can't face up to Christmas. They get to thinking about not having real homes and they get to feeling sorry for themselves. Some of them get drunk, some of them turn nasty, and some of them just wander off into a world of their own. That's what I mean about things getting squirrely around here at Christmas.

14

"But like I told you." Babette lowered her voice to a hush. "I was walking Josephine night before last. And when I passed the Star, I saw a small, bright light in a dark window. It went off and on three times. Then a truck pulled up in front of the building and a man came out the front door. He walked right over to the truck and picked up a small package. Then he hurried back inside.

"I didn't know that the light in the window had anything to do with the truck right then. But as Josephine and I passed by the Star on our way back from our little walk, I saw that same light in that same dark window again. This time it didn't blink. Instead, it made a path like a figure eight. Made it twice. Then suddenly Josephine and I got bumped good and hard by a young woman who rushed past us and into the Star. Poor Josephine began to cough, so I hurried her home right away."

"What do you think it meant?" Chase broke

in, swept up by Babette's story. Her stories were always better than books, and this one was off to a good start.

"Well, at first I was too worried with Josephine's coughing to give it much thought," replied Babette. "When an eighteen-year-old dog gets upset by a stranger, there's no telling what may happen to her. Josephine's okay but she's in a weak condition. I worry when she gets excited. That's why I always walk her in a baby stroller. She needs her air, just like anyone else. You'd think people would know not to bump into baby strollers!"

Babette was getting off on one of her favorite subjects: how cruel people were to animals. Chase knew he had to get her back on the track or he'd never get the whole story.

"Babette, I'm glad Josephine's okay," Chase broke in. "But what about those lights and the truck at the Star?"

"Well, it seems mighty strange to me,"

whispered Babette, "that the same thing, the very exact same thing, happened again last night when I was strolling Josephine. The lights blinked again. The truck pulled up. A man came down and got a package. And I saw the same figure eight made with the light in the same window. There was only one difference last night. After the figure eight appeared in the window, a tall young man rushed into the Star."

THE STAR HOTEL

"Babette, how about letting me walk with you tonight when you stroll Josephine past the Star?"

Babette was sure of Chase's interest now. "Meet me at the diner," she said. "We'll go from there after I feed the cats. That is, if your mother says it's okay."

That took the edge off Chase's excitement. "I'll work on her," he answered, not sounding very hopeful.

"Work hard," replied Babette.

3

A Close Watch
on the Waterfront

"WHY, MOM? Just give me two good reasons why I can't go with Babette to walk Josephine tonight."

"Chase, we've been through this before. Number one: I don't want you to go out on the street at night without a responsible adult . . ."

"But, Mom," Chase broke in, "Babette *is* a very responsible adult. She's more than twice as old as you are, and she's not scared of anything. Besides, she has Josephine for protection."

"Chase, Babette is 78 years old. And Josephine is hardly protection. I know how you feel about Babette. And Josephine. But neither of them meets my point number one."

Chase gave a heavy sigh, which his mother knew meant, *you* don't *know how I feel about Babette*.

His mother went right on. "Point number two: I don't want you to walk down Bleeker Street at night even with a responsible adult. That block next to the waterfront can be tricky, especially around the Star Hotel. Now if I'm not wrong, that's where Babette strolls Josephine. I know that's where she goes to feed the stray cats."

"Okay, Mom. You win. But why does everything that's fun have to be dangerous?"

There was no answer from his mother, who headed for the kitchen.

"I'll bet Dad would let me go if he was home," said Chase under his breath. Chase walked over to the telephone. "I'll have to call Babette and tell her the warden won't let me out on parole tonight," he muttered, hoping his mother would hear.

"Hello? . . . Is Babette there? I want to speak to Babette." Chase began to yell into the phone. "Tess, tell Babette I can't come out tonight. Did you hear that, Tess? . . . That's right, Tess. Just give Babette that message for me. 'Bye, Tess."

Chase hung up the phone and headed for the kitchen.

"What was all that yelling about?" his mother wanted to know.

"I called Babette to let her know I won't be with her tonight, and Tess answered the phone. She's half deaf. On the phone I think she's whole deaf."

"Oh, I see," his mother answered as she leafed through the *Evening Sun*. Suddenly she rattled the newspaper, folded it in half, and began to look at an article.

"Listen to this, Chase." She began reading out loud.

"You see what I mean, Chase? Right here, not two blocks away from where we live."

"Does it say anything else?" asked Chase eagerly.

"That's all," she replied. "I probably would have passed right over it if my eye hadn't caught some familiar street names."

Chase was getting the strangest feeling. Maybe Babette had stumbled onto something big. Maybe something dangerous. And Babette was out there right now. Out there in the midst of adventure.

4

Night Scare

THE ENTIRE evening was miserable for Chase. Nothing on TV seemed as exciting as what could be happening on the lower end of Bleeker Street. His mother spent most of the evening behind a book called *Future Shock*. Finally, Chase gave up and went to bed.

But sleep kept running away from him. Chase would doze and then wake up. He lost track of how many times. The sounds of trucks on the street seemed to cut right through his room. His throat was dry, and he needed to go to the bathroom.

"Might as well kill two birds with one trip," he mumbled as he started toward the bathroom. Halfway down the hall he fell over a sneaker and crashed against the wall. But his mother didn't seem to hear a thing.

Chase tiptoed from the bathroom into the kitchen. As he headed toward the refrigerator, a red light suddenly flashed through the room. It flooded the kitchen like a pulse—on and off. Chase thought about Babette and couldn't decide whether he was excited or afraid.

An ambulance was standing in front of the building, its red roof-top light still spinning around. Chase watched for a few minutes, but no one came out of the building. Probably a false alarm. He went back to bed and tried a trick Babette had once told him about.

"Here's a way to fall sleep," she had said.

"Hold a finger over your right nostril and breathe in through the left side of your nose. Then close the left side and breathe out through the right. Do this about ten times. Make believe you're floating on a cloud."

Chase had laughed at the time and said, "Who needs help falling asleep? Waking up is my problem."

Now he was breathing in one nostril and out the other. And floating on a cloud. It was working. Chase could feel his body growing limp and easy. Soon he was asleep.

Suddenly, the telephone rang, sounding sharp and loud in the hush of the late night. Chase sat upright in bed. He heard his mother's voice as she hurried for the phone. "Who in the world could be calling in the middle of the night?"

"Hello? . . . Chase went to bed hours ago. . . . Do you realize what time it is? . . . Who is this? . . . Tess? . . . Aren't you the lady who lives with Babette?" His mother was shouting into the phone now.

Chase was out of bed and at the phone by the time he heard Tess's name. His mother handed the phone to him. "Tess, what's wrong?" Chase yelled.

"Babette hasn't come home yet, and I'm getting worried. She's been gone for hours. Did you meet her, Chase?" Tess asked.

"No, Tess, I told you to tell Babette I couldn't meet her. Remember? Hold on a minute, Tess."

Chase put his hand over the phone. "Mom, Babette's missing. What should we do?"

"Tell Tess to call the police. If she has trouble explaining things, I'll talk to them."

With a shaky voice, Chase gave Tess the message and then hung up. Babette was out there somewhere, and there was nothing at all that he could do.

5

A Missing Person

SATURDAY morning meant a late breakfast. This was usually a nice time when they all talked over things that got put off during the week with the rush of getting to work and to school.

This Saturday morning was different, though. Everything was different since that phone call from Tess last night. Chase wanted to tell Mom what he knew about Babette and the Star Hotel. But he was afraid she wouldn't let him look for Babette if she knew everything.

"I'm sure the police will locate her. Maybe they already have," his mother said.

Chase played with the scrambled eggs on his plate. "Then why hasn't somebody called us?" he asked.

"Chase, why don't you go to the movies with Robert today?"

"Okay, Mom. I'll call Robert. But first I've just got to call Tess and check on Babette."

Chase dialed the phone and waited. He let it ring until he had counted seven times. Then he slowly hung up.

"That's funny—nobody answers. Tess hardly ever goes out."

"Try Robert before *he* goes out," called Mom as she began clearing away Chase's half-eaten breakfast.

In a few minutes Chase returned to the kitchen. "I'm meeting Robert at his house in an hour. He wants me to see his terrarium before the movie." Chase knew his mother liked him to run around with someone his own age for a change.

"That sounds nice, Chase. I'll do the shopping while you're at the movie. Then I'll meet you back here around two-thirty. Okay?"

Chase didn't answer. He was deep in his own thoughts. Thoughts and worries about Babette.

"Chase, did you hear me? Try to be back by two-thirty."

"Sure, Mom. Two-thirty."

"Chase, stop worrying. Babette will turn up, and she'll probably have some wild tale for you."

Chase didn't go the usual way to Robert's. Instead, he went by the old apartment house on Bedford Street where Babette lived. He pushed the bell marked B. BRELL several times. But there was no return buzz to show that anyone was at home.

"Where could they be?" muttered Chase. Then, as he turned to leave the building, there was Tess.

"Tess! Tess, have the police found Babette?" Chase shouted out.

Tess just shook her head. Chase could see the old woman had been crying. He also noticed that Tess was wearing her hearing aid and he was thankful for that. Tess dragged her heavy body toward a bench in the lobby. She sat down, looking old and tired and scared.

"Tess, I called this morning, but nobody answered," Chase said.

Tess pulled herself together a bit and began to tell Chase what had happened. "I was at the police station. They wanted a picture of Babette. A lot of the officers around here know her, but they wanted a picture and a description of what she was wearing when she went out last night. Sergeant Williams told me not to worry. They're searching the whole neighborhood. . . ."

"Babette knows how to take care of herself," Chase said. "Did she have Josephine with her?"

"Yes, but they've been gone for over twelve hours now. I just don't know. I just don't know what to do," said Tess, breaking into tears again.

"Get back to the apartment and stay by the phone, Tess," urged Chase.

As Tess stepped into the elevator, Chase added, "Now don't worry, Tess. The police are looking for Babette, and I've got an idea I want to check out myself."

As the elevator door closed, Chase rushed out the front door and headed straight for Bleeker Street.

6

Clue at the Diner

IT WAS mid-morning, but the street was almost empty. Bleeker Street doesn't wake up till the afternoon. Then it really comes alive at night. Chase hurried along until he reached the abandoned diner.

The diner cats were nowhere in sight. Usually they dashed out of the diner and into the street when a friend came by. And Chase was a friend. But now only Timid Freddy, who lived on the roof of the diner, could be seen. Timid Freddy ran along the roof, meowing to Chase.

"Where's the gang?" Chase called to Timid Freddy. "Where's Peg and Butterfly and the new kittens?"

"Back here with me," a voice answered from behind the diner. Peg, Butterfly, Dodger, and a half-dozen other cats were gathered around a middle-aged lady. It was Mrs. Leslie with her blond hair done up in large plastic curlers. Mrs. Leslie was the Saturday morning cat lady. Saturday was her day to feed the diner cats. As she poured fish-head stew into some old pans, there was the usual bedlam. Peg batted a kitten for tipping over his plate of stew. Dodger ran from plate to plate, unable to make up his mind.

"Mrs. Leslie!" called Chase over the noise of the cats. "Have you seen Babette?"

"No, darling. Yesterday was Babette's day. This is Saturday, my day. Babette never comes on Saturday. She hates my fish stew anyway. Says it stinks. Mighty high and mighty, she is. But look at old Peg go at those fish heads. The proof of the pudding is in the eating, I always say . . . ."

"Please, Mrs. Leslie, listen. Babette has been missing since last night. The police are looking for her."

"Missing? Babette missing? Run through that again, Chase."

As quickly as he could, Chase brought Mrs. Leslie up to date about Babette. But he carefully left out any details about the Star Hotel.

"I thought I'd check the diner to see if Babette really came by here last night," said Chase.

"How are you going to tell that?" asked Mrs. Leslie.

"Babette always feeds the cats on blue paper plates. If she came here last night, there ought to be some blue paper plates still here."

Mrs. Leslie and Chase looked around the diner area, but there were no paper plates. Or

any other containers except the pans Mrs. Leslie
had brought.

"I guess my hunch was no good," said Chase.
"Maybe she didn't even get this far last night."

"Of course there wouldn't be any paper plates
this morning!" piped Mrs. Leslie. "I must be
getting a little crazy. Dora always comes here
early Saturday morning and cleans up the place.
Dora can't stand a mess, so all the plates and

empty cans and trash go out with her. . . ."

"Wait a minute!" called Chase as he ran to the opposite end of the diner. He climbed up a short ladder that leaned against the diner. Timid Freddy came meowing over. On the roof was a blue paper plate, held by a rock to keep it from blowing off.

"She was here!" called Chase. "Look, Mrs. Leslie. Look! Babette always puts Freddy's food up here because he's afraid to come down and eat with the other cats. Dora must have missed this one. It means Babette was here, all right."

Mrs. Leslie looked at the blue plate. "Let's go tell the police about this," she whispered. "It might be a real helpful clue."

"No, wait, Mrs. Leslie," urged Chase. "Let's check out the diner first."

"It's wide open. You can see right through it. What's to check?" asked Mrs. Leslie.

"You can't see into the cellar," answered Chase.

"Nobody's ever been down there. I don't think there's a real cellar there anyway. The cats come and go, but I don't think there's anything under the diner but a little crawl space. I've never seen any door," explained Mrs. Leslie.

"There just might be a cellar down there," Chase replied. "Babette said that's where Butterfly had her kittens. Come on, Mrs. Leslie. Let's see if we can find an entrance to the cellar."

"It smells terrible in there," said Mrs. Leslie, holding back.

"It's not so bad in the winter. Come on, please, Mrs. Leslie!"

"Oh, all right. I guess nothing can happen in broad daylight. Go on, I'm right behind you, Chase."

Chase and Mrs. Leslie began to search every inch of the diner floor.

"If there's a cellar under here, there's got to be a trap door to it," Chase reasoned.

"Yeah, and if there's a cellar under here, it

41

must have been used to store supplies," added Mrs. Leslie. "And supplies are usually handy to the cooking area," she went on.

"I'll look behind the counter," called Chase as he headed in that direction.

Old pieces of linoleum were piled behind the counter. Chase began clearing them away.

"You were right, Mrs. Leslie!" he cried. "Here's a trap door, right next to the old refrigerator! Come on, help me get it open."

"No, now hold on a minute, Chase. Let's think this over. We could go get the police and let *them* open the trap door. There's a law about breaking and entering, you know."

"Mrs. Leslie, we've already entered, and we didn't have to break anything. The place is always wide open. What harm is there in pulling up the trap door?"

Mrs. Leslie came over slowly. "Well, I don't know, Chase."

"Please, Mrs. Leslie, just give me a hand."

42

Together they pulled at a rusty metal ring attached to the trap door. It made a sound almost like a groan, as it pulled back on its hinges.

The sunlight streaming into the diner didn't reach as far as the trap door. All Chase and Mrs. Leslie could see was a black hole, with dusty steps disappearing into the darkness below.

As they stared down into the dark hole, a scraping noise and a grunting sound floated up to their surprised ears.

7

Mental Messages

"I'M GETTING out of here!" yelled Mrs. Leslie. She grabbed Chase's hand and began dragging him out of the diner.

"Wait, Mrs. Leslie. It sounds like somebody's groaning down there!"

"I can hear it. That's why I'm getting out. And you're coming with me!" she said.

"But it might be Babette," begged Chase. "I've got to go down and look."

"Chase, the police should handle groaning noises in diner cellars. We're *both* going to the police. I'm not leaving you here alone."

"Mrs. Leslie, I've got to see if Babette's down there—now! It's creepy, but I've just got to look. Please stay here for just one more minute."

Chase didn't wait for an answer. He hopped down the short flight of dusty steps. The grunting and scraping sounds grew louder. And so did the thumping of Chase's heart.

"Babette, are you down here?" he called nervously in the dark. Once he reached the bottom, a ray of sunlight came in through the small opening the cats used to enter the cellar. It was about as much help as a weak flashlight.

Now the sounds were coming from under the staircase. Chase swallowed hard, took a couple of steps, and looked under the stairs. His eyes were used to the dark now, and he could see a figure clearly. It was Babette!

"Babette! Babette!" Chase cried as he began pulling a gag from her face. "Are you all right?"

Babette was tied to a chair. He began untying

the cords that bound her hands and feet.

Babette cleared her throat and tried to recover her voice. "I'm frozen!" she said. "Thank God you found me, Chase. I've been sending you strong, mental messages since last night. I knew you'd come. I just knew it. . . ."

"Mrs. Leslie! Mrs. Leslie!" shouted Chase. "Come, help. It's Babette. I've found her!"

Mrs. Leslie appeared at the top of the steps. "Is she dead?" she whispered.

"No, no, she's okay! Come on down," he yelled. I need help getting her out. He could hear Mrs. Leslie start down the steps.

Chase had the cords off Babette's hands and was working on the ones around her feet. Babette began rubbing her stiff hands together to get them warmed up.

"How did you get down here, Babette? Who tied you up? What were they up to? Did you know who they were?" Mrs. Leslie couldn't stop asking questions long enough to get answers.

"Never mind all that, Leslie. Just help me out of this awful place!" snapped Babette.

Together, they got Babette to the top of the steps.

"We've got to call the police. We've got to call Tess. I'd better call my Mom," Chase said.

"Yes, the police," echoed Mrs. Leslie. "I keep saying we should get the police."

Babette looked worn out. She had a sore red mark where the gag had rubbed against her face.

"Let the victim speak!" shouted Babette. She seemed to be more like the old Babette again. "I've been tied in a chair down in that cellar for what seemed like forever and I've had plenty of time to think. Give me a few minutes to get my blood going and I'll be all right. Then, Chase can walk me over to the police station. I've got a few things to report to those gentlemen."

"I'll go with you, Babette," offered Mrs. Leslie.

"Thank you, Leslie, but you could be a lot more help if you'd drop by and let Tess know I'm okay. She must be worried sick."

"Sure, of course," answered Mrs. Leslie, sounding disappointed not to be going to the police station, too.

Suddenly Chase remembered something.

"Babette, where's Josephine? Is she still down in the cellar?"

"No, Josephine's not in the cellar. Josephine is being held as a hostage."

8

The Key Witness

CHASE AND Babette stood before the policeman at the front desk, just inside the police station.

"No. For the last time, officer, I don't want to state my complaint," said Babette. "I just want to speak to Sergeant Williams. It's very private."

"But, lady, we have to fill out this form before you can speak to anyone," answered the policeman. "Now what is your last name?"

"Young man, will you *please* tell Sergeant Williams that . . ."

Before Babette could finish her sentence, a young policeman called from across the room. "Hey, lady, are you Miss Babette Brell? You sure answer to the description we put out last night for Miss Brell."

"Well, yes. Yes, I am Miss Brell, but . . . ah . . . but . . ." Babette began to stutter. "But I want to speak with Sergeant Williams. He knows me. And I'm not talking to anyone but him."

Chase was beginning to get nervous. He wished Babette would take it easy with the policemen.

"All right, Miss Brell, we'll send for Sergeant Williams. He's across the street having lunch." He turned to the policeman who had recognized Babette. "Patrolman Warren, would you go across the street and tell Sergeant Williams about the situation here?"

The phone rang, and the desk policeman

answered. Babette whispered to Chase, "Don't tell them anything. Wait till Sergeant Williams gets here." Chase nodded.

Soon Sergeant Williams, a big, booming man, burst through the door. "Babette, what do you mean giving us a scare like this? What have you been up to? Come on in my office and tell me all about it."

He swept Babette toward his office. Chase followed along. Sergeant Williams didn't notice him until they entered the room.

"What can I do for you, son?" said Sergeant Williams.

"I'm with Babette," Chase answered.

"Well, Babette, the report didn't say you were missing with a kid."

"Sergeant Williams, I was kidnapped, tied up, and my dog is missing. Chase Bellardo—this *kid*—saved my life. And there's more. Now, do you want the details?"

"Wait, wait, wait! Start at the beginning,

Babette. And just take it easy. We'll send for some coffee, and you can tell me everything."

"Could you get a side order of toast with that coffee?" asked Babette.

Babette started at the beginning. The Star Hotel. The strange lights. The truck. The person who rushed into the building and bumped into Josephine's stroller. Chase thought she'd never get to the part of the story that was new to him.

But finally Babette said, "Last night, I stopped by the diner and fed the cats as usual. Then Josephine and I strolled on down Bleeker Street, just the way we do every night. This time, we walked on the opposite side of the street from the Star. I wanted to get a better view of that window I told you about.

"The same truck I'd noticed before was already in front of the Star. I took Josephine out of her stroller and let her sniff around, so I could watch a bit. While Josephine was sniffing at a pizza crust in the gutter, a man got out of the truck and headed for the Star. He must have seen something he didn't like then, because he turned around as soon as he reached the hotel door. He dashed across the street, straight toward me and Josephine, and he threw a small package into Josephine's stroller. Then he took off toward the waterfront."

"What kind of package?" asked Sergeant Williams.

"Well, it was wrapped in dirty old cloth and tied with rope. I was afraid to check it out right in front of the Star. So I put Josephine back into the stroller with the package. Then I started wheeling her home. But just as we were passing the diner, I heard someone running behind me."

"Did you see who was behind you, Babette? Was it the same person who threw the package into Josephine's stroller?" Sergeant Williams asked.

"I didn't exactly see him. But I could *feel* that it was the same person. I could tell. I started going as fast as I could with the stroller. But the footsteps were gaining fast. By the time I was next to the diner, the footsteps were right behind me. Then I felt a strong arm around my neck, and a mean voice said, 'Keep moving into the diner!' "

Babette stopped to finish her coffee. Sergeant Williams was busy writing down notes on a pad. Chase thought he'd burst if she didn't hurry on with the story.

"Well, I was shoved and pushed—stroller, Josephine, and all—right into the diner. The mean voice said I shouldn't make a sound. I was so scared, I don't think I *could* have made a sound. Josephine must have been scared, too. She didn't bark—she just whimpered a little and hid in her stroller.

"It was dark in the diner and I couldn't see very well, but the person looked like the one who threw the package. He was a tall, thin man with dark hair and a black mustache. As quick as you please, he put a gag over my mouth. He pulled up the old trap door with one hand and held me with the other. He seemed to know the place well. Then he pushed me down the stairs into that prison. He tied me to a chair and said my old cat lady friends would probably find me in the morning. That's exactly what he called us—cat lady friends. Thank goodness for a warm December this year, and my fur neckpiece. I could have frozen."

Sergeant Williams asked the question that was on Chase's mind. "What happened to Josephine and the stroller and the package?"

"The man said he was taking Josephine with him. And I'd be getting a note about what to do next. He made some crack about how easy I'd be to spot. He said if I didn't follow directions, something would happen to Josephine."

Babette sounded tired now. Tired and close to tears.

Chase dug into his pocket and found a

Kleenex for Babette. She blew her nose and started to speak again. "The last thing I heard was the stroller bumping across the floor of the diner, and Josephine coughing. Then everything was quiet."

"You won't believe this, Sergeant, but I sent mental messages to Chase all night. And somehow he found me. All of a sudden, there was Chase pulling that awful gag from my face."

Sergeant Williams started to speak, but he was cut short by a knock on the door. "Yes?" he called. "What is it?"

The desk policeman opened the door a bit and poked his head in. "Sergeant Williams, there's a woman on the phone reporting a missing kid. She says he didn't show up at a friend's house, and that was over three hours ago."

"Why are you telling all this to me? You know how to handle missing persons." Sergeant Williams sounded annoyed.

"But Sergeant, the woman says the missing

kid is ten years old, wears glasses, has brown hair, and has on a Kid Power sweat shirt. The description just happens to fit the kid you have right here in your office."

9

A Plan Is Made

"I'M REALLY in for it now!" said Chase.

Sergeant Williams spoke to the desk police-man. "Have the call transferred here. I'll speak to Mrs. Bellardo." Then he turned to Chase and Babette. "You and Babette have stumbled onto something we've been trying to track down for a long time, Chase. I want to keep you here a little longer. But I'll explain everything to your mother and help get you off the hook."

The phone on Sergeant Williams's desk rang sharply.

"Hello? Mrs. Bellardo, this is Sergeant Williams. Your son is okay. . . . Yes. He's here with me at the Tenth Street Station. He's perfectly all right. He found Babette and she's all right, too. . . . No, you don't need to come down. I'll send him home in about fifteen minutes. Yes, I'll tell him you're upset. But please, Mrs. Bellardo, he's fine. . . . Yes, Mrs. Bellardo, in about fifteen minutes. . . . I will, Mrs. Bellardo. Thanks."

The policeman hung up the phone and turned to Chase. "It's okay with your mother. I told her you'd be home soon. Now, I have to talk very seriously with you and Babette. I'm sorry in a way that you're mixed up in this mess. But you are, and you just might be the key to help us crack the case. Right now, you're our only lead."

"What case? Stop talking in riddles and tell us what you mean." Babette was getting tired and annoyed.

"Well, Babette, I think you've been the first to

meet up with the ring of counterfeiters we've been trying to crack. We know they moved into the neighborhood about two weeks ago, but we haven't been able to learn anything further. That package in Josephine's stroller is just the kind of evidence we've been looking for . . ."

Babette cut in. "What evidence, Sergeant? I'm too tired to figure things out. Just tell me what you're talking about."

"Fair enough, Babette. We know that fake money is coming into the area. I think that's what was in the package that landed in Josephine's stroller. You were in real danger, Babette. And you might still be. The people in this business aren't playing games . . ."

Babette broke in again. "Count me out. I don't like the way these guys play. I've had enough."

"I promise that the police will protect you," Sergeant Williams said firmly.

Babette still was not sure.

"What about Josephine? Don't you want to get Josephine back?" asked Sergeant Williams.

Chase could see that the policeman had hit on something important to Babette.

"You're right, Sergeant. They've got Josephine. And I've got to get her back. And soon. Even if I could depend on those crooks being kind to animals, how could they know Josephine likes chocolate-covered doughnuts? In fact, she goes on a hunger strike unless she has at least one every day. . . ."

"Sure, Babette," said Sergeant Williams. "We've got to find Josephine. And that means finding our criminal."

Chase's mind was racing in a dozen directions. The Star must be the headquarters for the gang. The lights in the window must be signals they use. A sudden worry cooled Chase's excitement. What was his mother going to say when he got home?

Sergeant Williams pulled Chase back to the events of the moment. "Now, Babette, I want you and Chase to listen to me. Very carefully. Tomorrow is Christmas. And we have reason to believe that a big shipment of counterfeit money is going to come into the area. From what we already know and what Babette has told us, we think the gang will try to unload it at the Star Hotel."

"What's that got to do with us? And with Josephine?" asked Babette.

64

"As I was saying, Babette, tomorrow is Christmas, and we believe a big shipment will be smuggled in. Now if Bleeker Street and the Star Hotel are crawling with cops, we just might scare off the smugglers. But if an old lady was strolling along Bleeker Street, nothing would look unusual. Get me?"

Chase was ready to say, "Yes, I get you," but Babette cut in first.

"No, I don't get you, Sergeant. How is one old lady going to do anything about a gang of smugglers? I've already met up with a member of that gang, and I ended up bound and gagged in a cellar overnight. No, I don't get you."

"They've used you once to get money out of the Star Hotel. That's what I believe happened last night. Now here's what we're going to do."

Sergeant Williams spent about five minutes explaining very carefully how he wanted Babette to help the police on Christmas Day. Babette looked worried when he had finished. But Chase was excited about the plan. He wished he could play a part, too.

10

All Is Not Well

"Mom, I'm really sorry I scared you. I should have called. But so many things happened, I didn't get a chance."

"Chase, sit down," his mother said very quietly.

From the sound of her voice, Chase could tell they were going to have a serious talk.

"I'm glad you found Babette," said his mother. "I want you to know that so you'll understand the rest of what I'm going to say."

Chase had a sinking feeling in his stomach.

He remembered that he hadn't eaten lunch, but it wasn't hunger that was bothering him now. It was that awful feeling that he'd let Mom down. And he couldn't have picked a worse time. Mom was already upset that Dad wasn't going to make it home for Christmas.

"Chase, you're off on your own a lot now, so we have to put a great deal of trust in each other. You have to trust me, and I want to be able to trust you. So when you tell me you're going to Robert's house and then to the movies, I expect that's what you're going to do. It's not that I want to check up on you every minute . . ."

"Mom, I know I was wrong. But when I met Tess and she told me Babette was still missing, I just had to check out the diner. Remember, she asked me to meet her there last night? After that, so many things happened, I forgot the time."

"I know you did. And I'm not going to make a big deal about this one time." His mother sighed, and Chase knew she had something else

on her mind. Finally she said, "I wish you wouldn't spend so much time with Babette."

"Mom, I really meant to see Robert today, but . . ."

"Okay, Chase. Let's make a new deal. Tell me I can trust you to go where you say you're going and to return at the time we agree. Then I won't bring all this up again. Is it a deal?"

"It's a deal, Mom. I promise." Chase felt a

great wave of relief. The lump in his stomach seemed to melt away, and real hunger took its place.

"Could I have a bologna sandwich and some milk, Mom?"

"Come on. You must be starved. I'll have one, too. And you can tell me all the details." Chase's mother seemed relieved to have the serious talk over, too.

Chase spent the rest of the afternoon in his room trying to read a chapter in *Purple Planet People*, a science-fiction paperback. But he had a hard time staying with the purple people. He gave it up, wandered into the living room, and tried to find something on TV. Nothing much to interest him there. Back to the bedroom. Even though it was only five o'clock in the afternoon, Chase flopped on the bed. Then he realized how tired he was.

Sleep came quickly. But so did strange dreams. At first the dreams were all cloudy, but soon they began to clear up. In the dream Babette was driving a Santa Claus sled high over Bleeker Street. She was racing along at great speed, toward the rooftop of the Star Hotel. Her blue cape was trailing wildly in the wind. And who was leading the reindeers? Not Rudolph. A young, prancing Josephine, with brightly colored Christmas balls dancing from her poodle tail, was leading the way. The sled was filled with mysterious bundles all covered up and tied with strong rope. No brightly colored Christmas ribbons or holiday wrapping paper on any of those packages. Suddenly a light flashed from the chimney of the Star. It looked like colored smoke rings puffing out of the chimney. Josephine came to a dead stop, and all of the reindeer behind her stacked up like dominoes. Babette picked up one of the mysterious bundles and threw it down the chimney of the Star. Then everything suddenly exploded as if the chimney had become a volcano . . .

71

"Babette! Josephine! Babette!" screamed Chase. A light snapped on in the room. Mom was bending over the bed. She had her hand on Chase's forehead. "Chase, wake up. You're having a nightmare. It's all right now. It was just a dream. Just a dream."

Chase sat up and let her hold him for a moment. Then the sound of the door buzzer cut sharply through the apartment, and they both jumped.

"I'm not expecting anyone. Are you, Chase?" his mother asked.

"No, Mom."

The sound of the buzzer continued. Mom walked quickly to the button on the kitchen wall and buzzed back. Then she opened the door a crack, with the chain still on. Footsteps came bounding up the stairs.

"Who is it?" she called.

"Special delivery," came back the answer. "Does a Mr. Chase Bellardo live here?"

"Yes," she answered, opening the door all the way.

A young man holding out a pad and pencil said, "Sign here, lady. I've got a million other packages to deliver. Christmas is worse than ever this year. Thanks, lady. Here's the package. Merry Christmas."

"Merry Christmas," called Mom as she closed the door. Chase came into the living room. "It's for you, Chase."

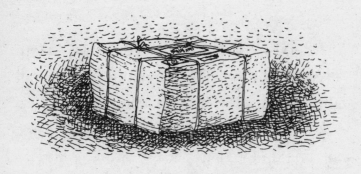

Chase pulled away the wrapping paper and there was a box with string around it. Inside the box was some more paper, and a smaller box. Then inside that box, yet another even smaller box. Finally, inside the third box, there was a check and a note.

"Well, what does the note say?" asked Mom.

" 'Buy yourself something special. I really miss

you and Mom. Merry Christmas. Love, Dad,' "
read Chase.

"He'll be home before you know it." Mom
tried to sound cheerful.

Chase tucked the check and the note into his
pocket and started back to his room.

Mom called, "Hey, Chase, how about us
having a Chinese dinner tonight? It's Christmas
Eve. Tomorrow's the start of a solid week of
turkey, so let's have something different tonight.
I can call the take-out place. We'll have wonton
soup, fried rice, and sweet and sour pork. How'd
you like that?"

"Mom, you're the greatest!" shouted Chase.
"Just don't forget the egg rolls."

11

Waiting for a Signal

CHASE woke up late the next morning. The clock on the table beside his bed said it was nine o'clock. For a moment he lay there, confused about the time. Why hadn't his mother called him? He was going to be late for school. Then he realized that it was Sunday, and Christmas Day, too.

"Oh, no," he said out loud. "Mom's gift!" He had forgotten to take her present into the living room last night.

He hopped out of bed, searched through his

chest of drawers, and pulled out a small package. Then he tiptoed into the living room. Luck was with him. Mom wasn't there. Chase placed his package on the coffee table next to a large gift-wrapped box.

"Chase, are you up?" his mother called from the hall.

"I overslept. Why didn't you wake me?" he answered.

"I figured you'd had a pretty full day, and a little extra sleep wouldn't hurt. Anyway, Merry Christmas, Chase."

"Merry Christmas, Mom," said Chase, picking up the small package and handing it to her.

"Should we open our presents now, or do you want some breakfast?"

"Presents first," he replied.

Chase and his mother sat on the sofa and peeled away the ribbons and paper. His mother finished first.

"My favorite perfume!" she exclaimed. "You

shouldn't have spent so much, Chase. Hey, what's this in the bottom? A deck of cards!"

"Look at the cards, Mom. They're not regular playing cards. They're old Tarot cards. Babette helped me find them. You can tell fortunes with these cards."

"Do I need a gypsy costume to make it work?" she asked, laughing.

"Come on, Mom. It's all very scientific. . . ."

"Come on, yourself, and get that box open. Or are you planning to ask the cards what's inside?"

Chase pulled open the top of the box, and there was a clear plastic bowl. With it came a package of soil, several packets of seeds, and a book of instructions.

"Wow! It's terrific! A terrarium! You can hang it up, too! This is much better than Robert's. His is square. Now we can both run experiments."

Chase began reading the labels on the seed packets. "I'm going to start breakfast, Chase," his mother said. "Come into the kitchen when you're ready."

"I just want to take a quick look at the instruction book," Chase answered. "Thanks, Mom. Wait till Dad sees this!"

By noon it was snowing lightly. Large, soft flakes floated past the windows.

Mom had the turkey in the oven and was settled down with a book. Chase had talked to Robert on the telephone about his new terrarium, and the two of them were already planning an experiment. It was a nice lazy day.

Except for one thing: Chase knew that Sergeant Williams was going to call Babette at three o'clock and tell her to start her stroll down Bleeker Street. Chase hadn't told his mother about the policeman's plan. And he hadn't told anyone that Babette was going to call him as soon as she got the go-ahead from Sergeant Williams.

As three o'clock drew nearer, Chase made

several visits to his room. The real purpose was to check the clock.

At 3:05 the phone rang. Mom picked it up on the first ring. It was Dad.

Mom talked on and on, and Chase was glad to see her smile and look so happy. But he worried about tying up the phone for so long. What if Babette tried to reach him and couldn't get through?

Finally, Mom gave the phone to Chase so Dad and he could talk. They wished each other Merry Christmas, and Dad promised to try to get home soon. Chase said he had a great adventure to tell him, but that it would keep until he could get home.

Mom took the phone again and talked for another few minutes. At last she said good-bye and hung up. It was past 3:30.

Chase went to his room but left the door open a crack—in case Babette called.

The house grew quiet. Mom dozed on the

couch. Chase stared out the window at the gently falling snow. Babette was out there. It was after four now. "I missed her call," he thought.

He tried reading the instructions for planting the terrarium. But he couldn't stick with the hard directions. He had the same trouble with another chapter of *Purple People Planet*.

By five, he couldn't stand it any longer. He covered Mom with a blanket. On a piece of Christmas wrapping paper he wrote:

I'll be back in a few minutes —
Chase

He placed the note on the coffee table in front of his mother. Then he slipped quietly out of the apartment and walked down to the street. His mother wouldn't mind if he walked around the block before dark, just to get some air.

When Chase stepped out into the street he couldn't believe his eyes. He looked hard through the snow. Yes, it was Babette coming down the block, pushing Josephine's stroller.

12

Tracking Down Josephine

BABETTE stopped before she reached Chase and began fixing the blanket in the stroller.

"You got Josephine back already!" cried Chase. "Why didn't you call me?"

Babette looked up. "No, the whole thing was changed. I got a note this morning saying that if I wanted Josephine back, I was to push an empty stroller past the Star at five-fifteen today."

"Does Sergeant Williams know about this?"

"Sure," answered Babette. He had to find a stroller for me on a Sunday, Christmas Sunday of all days. And he had to change the whole plan around. There was no time to call. Crazy crooks. What can you do? I just hope they can be trusted."

"Babette, I'm going with you," said Chase.

"You can't do that. What would Sergeant Williams say? What would your mother say? What . . ."

"Wait a minute. Don't you believe in fate, Babette? It was pure fate that caused us to meet right here, right this minute. It'll take only a few minutes to stroll over to Bleeker Street. And Sergeant Williams has got the whole place crawling with his undercover men. Why can't I go?"

Babette smiled. "I really can't ask you to come, much as I'd like to, Chase."

Chase was hurt and disappointed.

"But I don't know how I could keep you from tagging along after I've told you not to come," she added.

"We'd better start walking if we're going to be in front of the Star at five-fifteen," reminded Chase. "And I promised Mom I'd be right back."

Babette began pushing the stroller through the thin layer of snow that was sticking to the sidewalk. The street lamps shining on the white snow made yellow pools along the sidewalk. Babette and Chase had walked this way many, many times.

"Chase?" asked Babette. "Do you remember everything Sergeant Williams asked me to do? Go over it with me again. Okay?"

Chase began repeating Sergeant Williams's instructions as if he had gone over them a thousand times: "If you see the man who tied you up, you're to take out your handkerchief and blow your nose. Plainclothes police will be all along the street and inside the lobby of the Star Hotel. They'll be watching for the signal."

"Good, good," whispered Babette. "Now,

what did he say if I see the truck that brought those packages to the Star?"

"If you see the truck anywhere on the street, you're to push the stroller over to it and pretend you're tying a loose shoelace."

"Okay," said Babette, "that's it except for one thing. In case of an emergency . . ."

"In case of an emergency," Chase said, "You're to blow the police whistle on the chain around your neck. Not to be used unless there's big trouble," he added with a laugh.

"It all sounds so silly. Just like a bad movie," said Babette. "But it's real, Chase, so we've got to be careful."

They were nearing Bleeker Street. Babette and Chase stopped talking. It was only two blocks to the Star, and they needed to be alert for clues.

They passed a young man in black leather pants and jacket. Chase wondered if this could be one of the Sergeant's plainclothes police.

Babette was checking every truck parked on the street, looking for the one that delivered packages to the Star at night. They continued down Bleeker Street, on the opposite side from the Star, until they were past the old hotel.

"So far, so good," whispered Babette. "Let's cross the street and circle back in front of the Star."

Chase didn't say a thing. He just followed Babette across the street and started toward the entrance to the Star. An old woman stood outside the hotel. She looked like the bag lady bums Chase often saw in the neighborhood.

"Christmas gift! Give it here!" muttered the old woman as Chase and Babette came to a stop in front of the Star. The old woman reached out and tugged at Babette's fur collar.

"Christmas gift," she repeated. Babette pulled away.

Chase stepped into the doorway of the Star to get out of the snow, and almost got knocked into the street. The front door of the hotel suddenly opened outward, giving Chase a shove back onto the sidewalk. While the bag lady was chanting "Christmas gift" to Babette, a man stepped through the door. Quickly, he dropped a piece of paper into the stroller. Then he hurried down the street.

Babette was so annoyed by the bag lady that she didn't see the note or even notice the man who dropped it. But Chase did. He grabbed Babette's arm and started pulling her away from the Star.

"Come on, Babette," called Chase. He picked the slip of paper out of the stroller and pulled Babette toward the street light a few steps away.

"Here, Babette," he said. "That guy who just left the Star dropped this piece of paper into the stroller."

"What guy? I didn't see any guy."

"Babette, a guy came out of the Star while the old bag lady was talking to you," said Chase.

"And he dropped this paper into the stroller."
Chase waved the paper at Babette. "Look, it's a
message."

Chase held the paper up to the light and read:

If you want your
dog, push the
stroller into the
Star. Take the
elevator to the
third floor,
Room 310. You'll
get instructions there
about getting your
animal back.

"What should we do?" asked Chase.

"This isn't a part of Sergeant Williams's plan,"
replied Babette. "We've got to save Josephine,
but I can't put you in danger like this. Chase,
you wait outside. I know Sergeant Williams has

the street covered, and the lobby of the Star, too. But I don't know about the third floor."

"Please, Babette," whispered Chase. "Let me go with you. You can't leave me out on the street. It might blow the whole thing."

Babette thought for a second. "No time to argue now. Okay, Chase, let's head into this den of iniquity together."

13

Risky Business

"WHAT'S A den of iniquity?" asked Chase. He and Babette were hurrying toward the front door of the Star.

"Someplace where no child of your age should be," answered Babette as they came face to face with the bag lady for the second time.

Boldly Babette opened the door to the Star and pushed the stroller toward the elevator. Chase followed close behind her. A sleepy desk clerk didn't ask any questions. The elevator was open and standing empty on the lobby floor. Babette pushed the stroller inside, and Chase stepped in behind her.

"Push 3," said Babette.

Chase pushed, the door banged closed, and the old elevator groaned its way slowly upward. They reached the third floor without any stops, and the door opened.

Babette pushed the stroller into the dimly lit hall.

"Get back in the elevator and keep your finger on the Hold button," whispered Babette. From inside the elevator Chase could hear sounds of record players and loud laughter. It felt squirrely to Chase. Suddenly, he knew what Babette meant when she had said the Star gets squirrely at Christmas time.

Babette pushed on down the hall. A door marked 310 opened, and it seemed as if the sound of a TV set had suddenly been turned up loud—too loud. A young woman in a long dress and shoes with six-inch platforms walked into the hall.

"Stay where you are," she said in an I-mean-business way.

Then a pair of hands reached out of the room—hands holding a large package tied with strong cord.

"Put this package under that blanket," ordered the woman in the platform shoes. "Then roll the stroller up Bleeker Street to the cat diner. There you'll change strollers with someone. Your dog will be in the stroller you get at the diner."

Babette started to say something. But the tall girl in the platform shoes cut her short. "No questions. Just do as you're told."

Babette backed into the elevator with the stroller. Chase pushed the button and the door rattled shut. He pulled the note from his pocket and tucked it under the package. The old elevator car creaked its way down to the lobby.

Chase and Babette went back through the lobby and out the front door. The bag lady came at them again. Babette paid no attention and headed the stroller in the direction of the diner.

"I don't like it," whispered Babette. "That woman on the third floor looked like the one who bumped into Josephine's stroller the other night."

"I wonder what's in the package," said Chase.

"I think we're being used," answered Babette. "If Sergeant Williams's hunch is right, we're moving a counterfeit fortune out of the Star right now for those crooks and dognappers. Where are all of those plainclothes officers who were supposed to be watching us every minute?"

"All I've seen is that crazy bag lady," answered Chase. "And here she comes, following us," he added.

Babette began walking faster. Chase ran along beside her. Soon the diner was in sight. They both slowed down a bit. The diner looked strange in the dim light and the falling snow. The holes in the broken windows looked like blind eyes staring into the night. As they came alongside the diner, a cat cried. Chase could see Timid Freddy walking on the rooftop, looking for a hiding spot out of the snow.

"Stick close to me," whispered Babette. Chase reached for her hand.

Suddenly a hard voice called, "Push the stroller behind the diner!" It was a voice coming from somewhere out of the dark. Chase and Babette could see no one. They stood in the snowy street, frightened and not moving.

14

Wrapping It Up

"AROUND HERE!" repeated the hard voice.

"We'd better move," whispered Babette.

Babette pushed the stroller around the corner of the diner. Chase followed a few steps behind. As he passed the open door of the diner, a shadowy figure grabbed him. A hand covered his mouth before he could make a sound. Chase and the figure vanished inside the diner as quickly and silently as one of the cats.

Babette rounded the corner and came face to face with a man holding a stroller. Even in the dark, Babette knew this was the hard-voiced man who had gagged her and kidnapped Josephine.

"Give me that stroller, and keep moving with this one," he growled.

Without a word, Babette switched strollers and moved toward the street again. For the first time, she realized that Chase was missing. Suddenly, she was more angry than frightened. She made a dash for the street, dragging the stroller with one hand and reaching for the police whistle with the other. She popped the whistle into her mouth and blew with all her might.

Everything seemed to happen at once. Light flashed into the diner. The bag lady ran around the corner of the diner with a gun in her hand, pointing it at the man with the stroller. "Hold it right there, Buster!" shouted the bag lady in a voice that sounded very much like a man's. "You're under arrest!"

100

A police car screeched to a stop outside the diner. Sergeant Williams and three other policemen jumped out.

A young man dressed in black leather pants and jacket stepped out of the diner holding a frightened Chase by the hand.

Babette was still blowing her police whistle. Just then a coughing sound came from the stroller. The whistle fell from Babette's lips as she bent to look inside. She lifted the blanket. There was Josephine. The old dog raised her head and looked up for the last time at Babette. Then she coughed again and dropped back into the blanket.

By the light of the street lamp, Chase saw the sad look on Babette's face as she pulled the blanket over Josephine's head.

Sergeant Williams was calling out orders to his officers. "Handcuff that man and bring the stroller over here. I think it has just the evidence

we need." He looked at the package and quickly read the note Chase had tucked under the cord. Then he called into a hand radio, "Go ahead with 'Plan Star.' Move into the third floor, room 310. Hold everyone for questioning." He clicked off the radio and looked around.

"Patrolman Warren, take off that silly wig," called Sergeant Williams to the bag lady who had arrested the man with the stroller. "Good work," he said.

Chase and Babette had been forgotten for a moment. Then the young man in the leather outfit came over.

"Sorry to scare you like that, kid. But you weren't supposed to be in our plan. I was afraid to let you go behind the diner where that guy was hiding with the dog. I knew I'd frighten you, but at least you'd be safe inside the diner."

Sergeant Williams walked over to Babette. "You've been a real trouper, Babette. We owe you more than I can put into words. I'm going to see that you and Chase get a merit citation from the police department. But it's over now, and you have Josephine back."

Babette didn't say a word. She just stood there in the snowy street with a faraway look on her face.

Sergeant Williams continued, "We'll send you both home now in a police car. You've had enough for one night. I'll have to see you and Chase tomorrow at the station for some details. And I suppose, Chase, I'll have to do some more explaining to your mother. Right?"

"Thanks," answered Chase. Babette still didn't say a thing.

"Sergeant Williams, could I walk Babette home? It's only a couple of blocks, and I think we'd rather walk," said Chase.

"Sure. But I'll have to send Patrolman Warren with you just to keep on the safe side."

"Thanks again," said Chase. He pulled on Babette's sleeve. She moved forward, pushing the stroller. Patrolman Warren followed a few steps behind them. When they reached the corner, Babette pulled a small plastic bag from her pocket and dropped it into a garbage can. Chase saw that it contained a chocolate-covered doughnut. Then Babette spoke. "Chase, you know, don't you? You know Josephine is . . ."

"Yes, I know," said Chase. "I'm sorry, Babette."

15

Out With the Old—
Ring in the New

Mom HAD slept through the whole thing. In fact it was Sergeant Williams's call that woke her. He explained the matter of Chase's meeting with Babette.

"I'm sorry your kid had to get mixed up in it. But, on the other hand, it was one of those lucky breaks," he explained. "If Chase hadn't found the note in the stroller, it might have blown our whole plan."

The morning papers carried a full story about the raid on the Star Hotel and the capture of some key figures in the counterfeiting ring. There were pictures of the tall woman with the platform shoes, the guy with the hard voice who had tied up Babette, and other members of the ring.

But there were no pictures of Chase or Babette. Sergeant Williams told the press about the important role "an outstanding senior citizen and a brave boy had played in breaking the case." But he refused to give their names to the reporters.

Chase and his mother had read the article so many times they knew it by heart. Now they read it again while they waited for Babette to come for lunch—a big breakthrough!

"Babette might have liked to see *her* picture in the paper," said Chase.

"How about you?" asked his mother.

"Me? Aw, no, I don't care about that kind of thing. Unless maybe Babette wanted me to pose with her."

"I'm kind of looking forward to meeting Babette," said Mom. "I guess I really should have gotten to know her before now."

"Mom, there's something I've got to tell you before Babette gets here. Josephine is dead."

"You mean they killed that poor dog?"

"Not exactly. But Josephine did die right after Babette got her back. She just coughed and stopped breathing."

"I'm so sorry," Mom said softly. "You said she thought the world of that old dog."

The buzzer rang.

Chase and Mom both jumped.

"I'm still a little edgy," said Mom. "That must be poor Babette."

Chase opened the door and Babette burst into the room.

Mom, who was expecting to see a little old lady overcome with sadness, could hardly believe her eyes. Babette was dressed in the strangest costume the second-hand shops along

Bleeker Street could sell. She looked like a Christmas tree with her long red dress, green velvet cape, and wild orange hair topped with a silver hat.

"Mrs. Bellardo, do forgive me for being late," cried Babette.

"It's quite all right," stammered Mom.

"I'll just flop on the sofa for a moment if you don't mind," said Babette.

When she stretched out full length on the sofa, Chase noticed her funny space shoes sticking out from under the long red dress. He burst into laughter.

"I can't help it," he cried. "Those shoes do it to me every time." Soon they were all laughing together.

Mom recovered a bit and said, "I was sorry to hear about Josephine. You must be heart-broken."

"Why, no," answered Babette. "Whatever makes you think that? I got Josephine back before she died, and that's what mattered to me. Josephine went out the way I'd like to go. A real hero, you might say. You know she was past her eighteenth birthday. I figure she was a hundred and twenty-six years old by human age. Now how many hundred-and-twenty-six-year-old folks do you know who live their lives right where the action is the way Josephine did?"

Chase and his mother were silent. They couldn't think of one.

"As I was saying," Babette continued. "I'm sorry to be late but I had to meet with the Director of the Friends of Man's Best Friend Society. He will see that Josephine is buried in the best pet cemetery. Josephine had style, and I'll have nothing but the best for her . . ."

The telephone rang.

Mom picked it up and answered. "Chase, it's Robert—for you."

"Robert, we've got company now so I'll talk to

you later. But the bet is on! . . . You said it!"

Chase hung up the phone.

"What's all this about a bet with Robert?" asked Mom.

"Now that we both have terrariums, Robert and I have a bet about who can grow the biggest plants. We're going to start with the same seeds, at the same time . . ."

Babette raised herself from the couch. "Listen, I know a secret way to make your plants winners."

"What is it?" asked Chase.

Babette lowered her voice, and said, "If you talk to your plants, sing to them, and tell them you love them, they'll do much better. You can't lose that way."

"Maybe Babette's idea works for people, too," said Mom. "Meantime, there's a Christmas turkey in the kitchen that's been waiting two days to be eaten."

While his mother was out of the room, Babette motioned for Chase to come over to the couch.

"As I was on my way over here today," she whispered, "the strangest thing was going on at the old Liberty Storage Warehouse on Bleeker Street. It's been boarded up for years, you know."

"Yes, I know," said Chase. "What was strange about it?"

"Well, a long black car, with a young woman in the back seat, pulled up in front of the warehouse. That rusty old warehouse door mysteriously opened. Then the car drove in and the door closed behind it."

"Well?" asked Chase.

"That's all. The big black car vanished inside the empty old warehouse."

Babette leaned closer to Chase. "I think we ought to stroll by there."

"When?" whispered Chase.

"What about tomorrow night?"

"Mom's still a little nervous. I'll have to think of a way to get out."

"Work on it," said Babette.

"I'll try," mumbled Chase.

"Try hard!" urged Babette.

WILLIAM H. HOOKS is director of the publication division of The Bank Street College and educational consultant for ABC-TV's children's programming. He is also the author of a number of articles and books for both adults and children, including *The New Extended Family* (co-authored), a book dealing with daycare in America today, *The Seventeen Gerbils of Class 4A*, and *Doug Meets the Nutcracker*.

Mr. Hooks grew up in rural North Carolina, the setting for his first novel, *Crossing the Line* (Knopf). He is a long-time resident of New York City.